ISBN: 978-1-0878-1106-2 (Hardcover)

Zoo See Me!

Zoo See Me!

Story by Chris Distler
Pictures by Timothy Williams

Ready for an adventure, boy?

Wonder what she can see from up there.

It's very nice to meet you!

Watch your feet, don't step on him!

Looks like fun, I want a ride!

What big teeth, I bet he's hungry.

Why is he hanging upside down?

Go on, go pick on somebody else!

We're too big to be your dinner!

Think she can breathe underwater?

He must think I'm pretty funny!

Hmm, I guess she's still sleeping.

Can that guy see where he's going?

Whoa, he looks just like me!

Hey now, be careful with that thing!

Time to go home. Goodnight, zoo.

Meet the Animals!

Dog

Dogs are not actually colorblind, but see things in shades of yellow, blue and grey.

Giraffe

Giraffes are the tallest land animals, standing 14-19 feet tall with 6-8 foot necks.

Elephant

Elephants have long trunks which they use for breathing, eating and grabbing things.

Mouse

Common mice are about 3-4 inches long with 2-4 inch tails.

Kangaroo

Female kangaroos have a pouch where they can carry their babies, called joeys.

Lion

Lions are carnivores, and eat between 11 and 15 pounds of meat per day.

Ring-Tailed Lemur

Lemurs have opposable big toes, so they can use their feet like hands to climb.

House Fly

Flies have compound eyes, so they see multiple images instead of just one.

Chameleon

Chameleons have independent eyes so they can look at two different things at once.

Hippopotamus

Hippopotamuses live on land and in water, and spend 3-5 minutes underwater at a time.

Hyena

Hyenas make a variety of vocal sounds, some of which sound like laughter.

Sloth

Sloths are more active at night, and sleep for up to 10 hours during the day.

Bat

Bats use echolocation, a type of sonar, to sense where things are around them.

Chimpanzee

Chimpanzees are the closest living relative to humans, sharing much of the same DNA.

Rhinoceros

Rhinoceroses have long sharp horns that are used for fighting and finding food.

Owl

Owls have extremely large eyes, which are perfect for seeing things at night.